BLUES SET

Contents

About the CD

The audio CD represents a live performance of the setlist by a four-piece group. The songs are played in the most standard, tried-and-true arrangements for guitar, keyboards, bass, and drums, remaining faithful (within reason) to the original versions. In order to cover the vocals as recorded, at least three—if not all—bandmembers should be able to sing. Listen to the recording as you practice your individual parts, paying attention to the feel and the sounds used.

Recorded by the Hal Leonard Studio Band at Beathouse Music, Milwaukee, Wisconsin.

Born Under a Bad Sign

Words and Music by
Booker T. Jones and William Bell

Intro

Moderately Slow Blues

Chorus

Born ___ un-der a ___ bad ___ sign. ___

Been down ___ since I be-gan to crawl.   If it was-n't for bad ___ luck,

you know I would-n't have no luck at all.   1. Hard luck and trou-ble
2., 3. *See additional lyrics*

been my on-ly friend. I've been on my own ___ ev-er since I was ten. ___

Chorus

Born ___ un-der a bad ___ sign. ___   Been down ___ since I be-gan to

To Coda

crawl.   If it was-n't for bad ___ luck   I would not a have no luck at all. ___

VOCALS • GUITAR • KEYBOARD • BASS • DRUMS

BLUES SET

The Performance Guide for Bands

CD Includes Full-Band Demonstrations

ISBN 0-634-03521-5

HAL•LEONARD® CORPORATION

7777 W. BLUEMOUND RD. P.O. BOX 13819 MILWAUKEE, WI 53213

Visit Hal Leonard Online at
www.halleonard.com

How to Use the Gig Guides

This book is laid out with performance in mind. The setlist we have included reflects a wide selection of the most accessible, "field-tested" material available, arranged for a four-piece band in a sequence that's meant to keep your audience entertained. Use it in rehearsal and performance, following along with the lead sheets and individual parts. Each song in the set includes:

- A lead sheet with chords, melody, and lyrics;
- An intro page with song facts, song form, and performance tips for the full band;
- A page of guidelines for each bandmember, including crucial parts and performance tips for vocals, guitar, keyboards, bass, and drums.

Song intro pages contain some information that might be useful to the frontperson as between-song banter: the story behind the song, when and by whom it was recorded, and so on. Parts and performance tips are written by professional musicians with field experience (not just some guy in a cubicle). If all bandmembers follow their parts in the book and the accompanying CD, and the band rehearses well, you will be gig-ready in no time.

Additional Lyrics

2. I can't read, I didn't learn to write.
   My whole life has been one big fight.

3. You know, wine and women is all that I crave.
   A big leg'd woman gonna carry me to my grave.

Overview

The blues is a distinctly American form of music whose evolution is as wide and diverse as the people who play it. "Born of slaves and performed for kings and queens," it transcends race, geography, and social order. No wonder it's as popular today as it ever was. The set outlined in this book represents both the modern and classic sides of the blues, a genre that continues to move and entertain audiences everywhere.

Our first number, "Born Under a Bad Sign," was written by Booker T. (Jones) and saxophonist Albert Bell. They wrote the song for blues guitar legend Albert King, who had a hit with it in the summer of 1967. It's been a must-know song for blues bands ever since.

Like so many—but not all—songs in the blues canon, "Born Under a Bad Sign" is about losing—being plagued by bad luck. The singer's job is to deliver the powerful lyrics and melody with conviction. The interplay between guitarist and singer is the backbone of the melodic movement; Albert King was a singing guitarist who would answer his vocals with emotional licks. The drums establish a loose groove, played behind the beat. The piano is comping an eighth-note pattern, also played "on the back side of the pocket." The bass carries the signature riff that repeats hypnotically throughout the tune. Note the song's odd form; listen closely and know when changes are coming. Unlike many 12-bar tunes, this one doesn't telegraph its pattern easily.

Before we start to burn, here are some things that should be in order for the live set:

- Monitors are set and pointed so that all band members can hear the singer easily.
- Everyone is in tune.
- Stage volumes are balanced and not overpowering the vocals.
- Stage lights are on, aimed, and not blinding the audience.
- Can everyone in the band be seen from the audience? Can you all see each other?

Section	Length	1st Chord
Intro	2 bars	C#7
Chorus	8 bars	C#7
Verse 1	4 bars	C#7
Chorus	8 bars	C#7
Verse 2	4 bars	C#7
Chorus	8 bars	C#7
Guitar Solo/Chorus	10 bars	C#7
Verse 3	4 bars	C#7
Chorus	12 bars	C#7

Lead Vocal

Range: E to G#

PERFORMANCE TIPS

- Sing with plenty of "umph," deep and slightly rough—bring out the frustration and sorrow in the lyrics.

- Slide into select notes on chorus ("*born* under a *bad* sign…").

- Add some extra grit on high notes ("been *down*…").

- Add vibrato on held notes at ends of phrases ("…wouldn't have no luck at *all*.").

- Sing full force on last line.

Guitar

Intro Lick

Chorus Lick

Guitar Solo

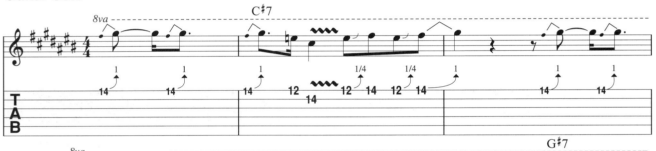

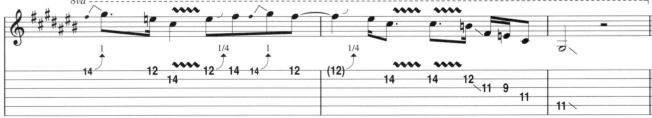

Ending Lick

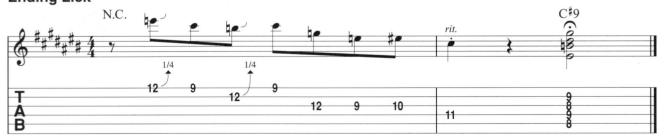

PERFORMANCE TIPS

- Use slight distortion.

- Attack strings aggressively with pick.

- Play lead licks throughout (no chords or riffs).

- Use C♯ minor pentatonic scale for licks.

Keyboards

Intro

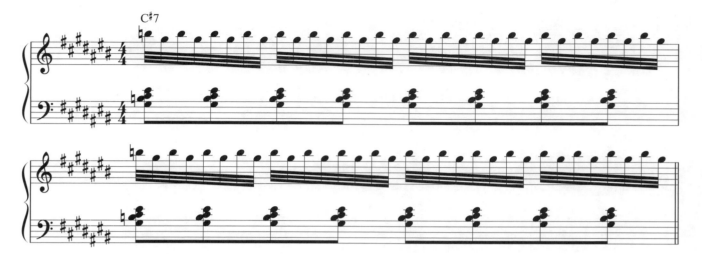

Chorus

PERFORMANCE TIPS

- Use an acoustic piano sound throughout.

- Play eighth-note staccato pattern for verse and chorus.

- Lock in with drums—especially hi-hat.

- Accent downbeats.

- Keep upbeats on verse almost imperceptible.

- Play intro trills at end of chorus 1 and guitar solo/chorus.

- Move chords up an octave on final chorus and coda.

Bass

Intro

Chorus

Verse

Ending

PERFORMANCE TIPS

- Play with fingers near the neck pickup for a full sound.

- Don't rush the phrases.

- Play notes for their full duration.

- Don't rush pickup notes into second four measures of the chorus.

Drums

Intro

Main Groove

Chorus Lick

Chorus Second Ending (Fill into Solo)

Chorus – 4th Measure after Solo

Ending

PERFORMANCE TIPS

- Band begins together with pickup fill.

- Main groove played on closed hi-hat; play ghost notes on snare for sixteenth shuffle feel.

- Play chorus lick every fourth measure of each chorus.

- Play ride on solo section.

- Band plays ending lick together; ritard last measure.

Killing Floor

**Words and Music by
Chester Burnett**

Intro
Moderate Blues

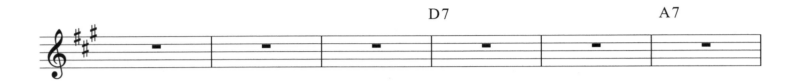

1. I should-'ve

Verse

quit you   a   long time a go.___   I should-'ve

2., 3. *See additional lyrics*

quit___ you, ba - by,   a   long time a - go.___

4th time, to Coda

You know, I would-n't be here___ now, peo - ple,   down___ on the kill-in'

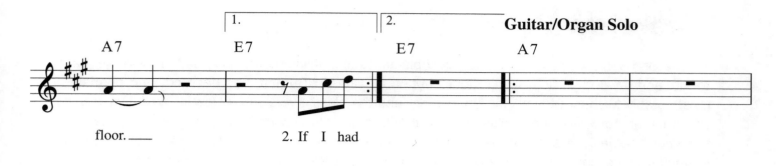

floor.____   2. If I had

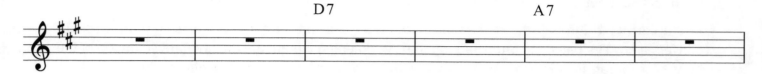

3. I should-'ve

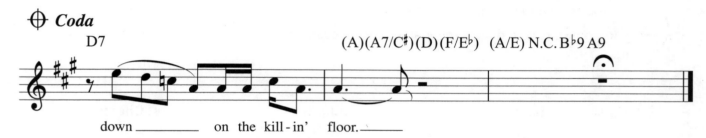

down ____ on the kill-in' floor.____

Additional Lyrics

2. If I had listened to my second mind,
   Oh, if I would've listened, baby, to my second mind,
   You know, I wouldn't be here now, people,
   Down on the killin' floor.

3. I should've gone when my friend said, "Come to Mexico with me," yeah.
   Oh, I should've gone when my friend said, "Come to Mexico with me."
   You know I wouldn't be here now, people,
   Down on the killin' floor.

4. Oh, I should've quit you, baby, a long time ago.
   Yes, I should've quit you, baby, a long time ago.
   'Cause you know, I wouldn't be here now, people,
   Down on the killin' floor.

Overview

The second song in our set is strategically placed for its infectious rhythmic pattern; it comes out rockin' and doesn't let up. "Killing Floor," written by Chester Burnett, has been covered by many, most notably Michael Bloomfield, Albert King, and the classic version by Howlin' Wolf. Lyrically, it tells another story common to blues tunes—that of a good love gone bad. The magic is in the way the singer carries the song. Again, conviction is the key. In the second verse he sings, "If I had listened to my second mind… I wouldn't be here now people, down on the Killing Floor." The lyrics warn us about not trusting our intuition—another universal theme in the blues.

In the intro, and through the rest of the song, the guitar and organ have a "call and response" conversation. The bass and drums are aggressive, keeping the energy and the groove on top of the beat. The organ is a Hammond B3-style with a Leslie rotating speaker effect. The guitarist is playing a Strat through a Fender Bassman amp (ideally). Both guitar and organ solos should be played with as much attitude as the players can muster. (Attitude and conviction are two words you may see much more in these pages.)

- Is the band playing with dynamics (getting quieter when the singer sings and when the solos start)?
- Does the singer sing with conviction?
- Are the bass and drums playing as one unit?
- Is the bassist playing the syncopated pattern evenly?

Section	Length	1st Chord
Intro	16 bars	E7
Verse 1	12 bars	A7
Verse 2	12 bars	A7
Guitar Solo	12 bars	A7
Organ Solo	12 bars	A7
Verse 3	12 bars	A7
Verse 4	12 bars	A7

Lead Vocal

Range: C# to F

PERFORMANCE TIPS

- Sing in a clean, strong voice.

- Add fast vibrato on phrase ends.

- Practice bluesy "melismas" on chorus, moving through many notes on one syllable ("*down* on the killing floor").

- Try to bring out the feeling of lament expressed in the lyrics.

Guitar

Intro

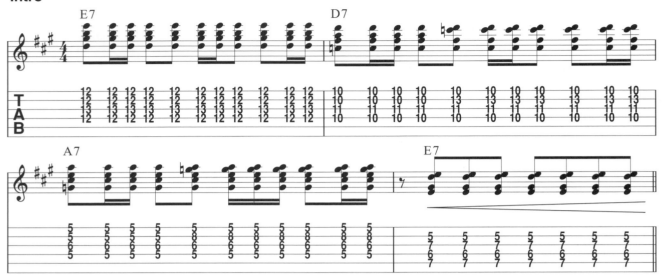

Intro/Verse Pattern

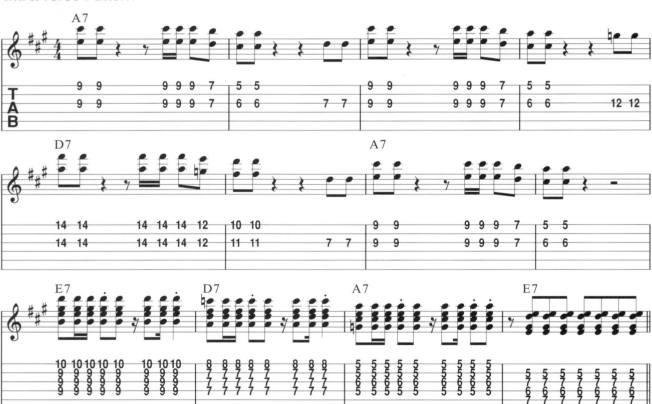

PERFORMANCE TIPS

- Use neck pickup with slight distortion.

- Play spaciously behind vocals.

- Play a spacious guitar solo using the A blues scale.

Keyboards

Comping Patterns

Organ Solo

PERFORMANCE TIPS

- Use Hammond B3 organ sound with fast Leslie speaker effect.

- Get off chords quickly.

- Add extra fills in higher register during guitar solo.

- On organ solo, alternate between minor and major thirds for the "blue note" effect.

- Create rhythmic tension on solo by pulling back on tempo, arpeggiating up, glissing up to higher trills.

Bass

Verse Pattern

PERFORMANCE TIPS

- Keep groove in the pocket.

- Play with a bouncy feel.

- Improvise variations on main line, but always keep original groove in mind.

- Dial in a richer tone that helps enunciate this busy part.

Drums

Main Groove

Verse Lead-in Fill   **Solo Lead-in Fill**

Coda/Ending

PERFORMANCE TIPS

- Song begins with guitar; band enters together at measure five.

- For solo lead-in fill, play snare slightly off-center with rimshots for a ringing sound.

- For solo section, play main groove on ride first time through, hi-hat the second.

- Song ends with band playing ending lick, kicking the "two-and."

Rock Me Baby

Words and Music by
B.B. King and Joe Bihari

Intro

1. Rock me, ba - by, rock me all ___ night long.___
2., 3. *See additional lyrics*

Rock me, ba - by,___ rock me all ___ night

long. ___ I want you to rock me, ba - by,___

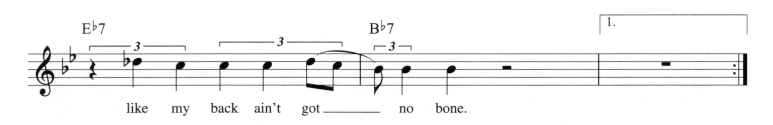

like my back ain't got ___ no bone.

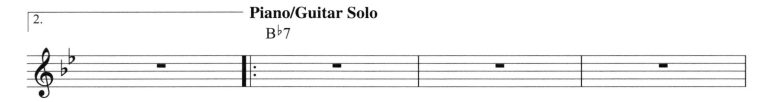

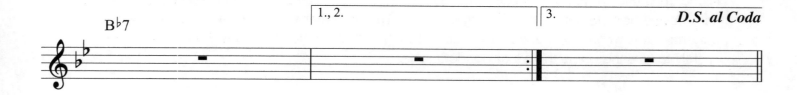

till I want no more. ———————— Oh, yeah. ——

Additional Lyrics

2. Roll me, baby, like you roll a wagon wheel.
   Roll me, baby, like you roll a wagon wheel.
   I want you to roll me, baby,
   You don't know how that makes me feel.

3. Rock me, baby, honey, rock me slow.
   Mm, rock me, baby, rock me, rock me real, real slow, yeah.
   I want you to rock me, baby,
   Till I want no more. Oh, yeah.

Overview

B.B. King, the undisputed King of the Blues, first recorded "Rock Me Baby" in 1964. It's a wonderful example of a traditional "Chicago blues shuffle," a style that takes years to truly master. Many young bands make the mistake of trying to play it with the same energy as a rock tune. Blues shuffles are best played "behind the beat," and that's what gives them their feel. To "rock it," or play it in front of the beat, makes it sound rushed. Relax, and concentrate on keeping it even and loose.

Lyrically, "Rock Me Baby" is a double entendre about dancing and loving. "I want you to rock me, baby, like my back ain't got no bone"—a stylization that makes the song what it is, a classic.

This style of traditional blues came from the jazz era, and the instruments naturally follow suit. The guitarist has switched to a thin hollow-body. The bassist (ideally) plays an upright bass. The keyboardist uses a grand piano sound and plays very loose. The piano solo is sparse and effective as a device used to set up the clean guitar solo. The drummer is playing a quiet "double shuffle" pattern; this is when both hands play exactly the same pattern, but the snare-drum hand is dragged slightly to give the whole thing that wonderful lope.

- The whole band's volume should come down right after the intro.
- Piano should be comping "way behind the beat."
- Is the bass steadily walking its quarter-note pattern?
- Does the first solo "set up" the second soloist?

Section	Length	1st Chord
Intro	4 bars	B♭7
Verse 1	12 bars	B♭7
Verse 2	12 bars	B♭7
Piano Solo	12 bars	B♭7
Guitar Solo	24 bars	B♭7
Verse 3	12 bars	B♭7

Lead Vocal

Range: D♭ to A♭

PERFORMANCE TIPS

- Sing in a light, breathy, "soft blues" voice.

- Sing behind the beat and drag your phrases out past the barline.

- Use dynamics for expressiveness: get louder on highest notes ("rock me *all* night long").

- Add slow, shimmery vibrato on ends of phrases.

Guitar

Intro

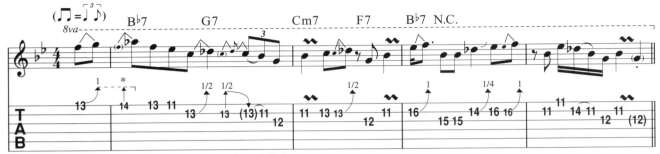

*While holding bend, add pinky on 14th fret.

Verse

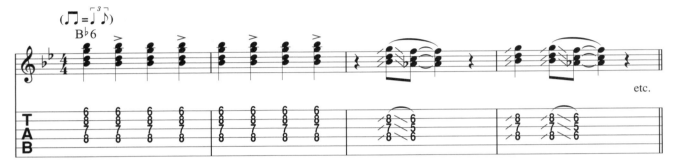

The "B.B. Box," key of B♭

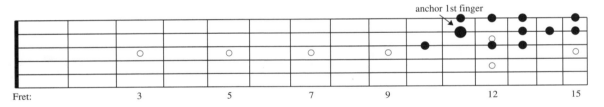

Fret: 3 5 7 9 12 15

Ending

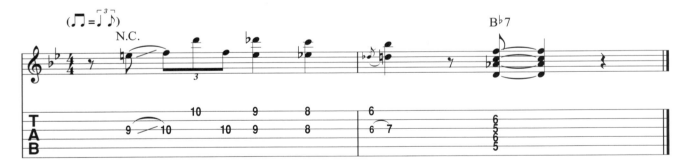

PERFORMANCE TIPS

- Use a semi-hollowbody (ES335-style) guitar.

- To really nail this sound, dial treble setting on amp to 10, bass to 2, midrange to 5.

- Lay back to produce a "lazy" shuffle feel.

- Use "B.B. Box" (above) for solos.

Keyboards

Intro

Verse

Left-Hand Voicings

Solo

PERFORMANCE TIPS

- Use acoustic piano sound throughout.

- Play chords with left hand, keeping right hand available for riffs.

- Accent chords with snare on two and four.

- Borrow fills from the country-jazz library.

Bass

Intro

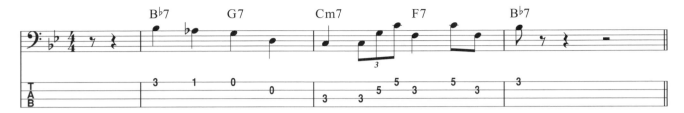

Verse Pattern

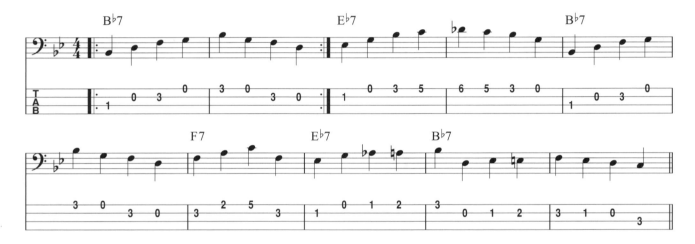

PERFORMANCE TIPS

- Play with a nice warm upright bass sound (or ideally an upright bass).

- Play quarter notes evenly.

- Walk the bass—envision yourself taking a stroll in the park with your nicest brand new shoes.

- Improvise on the walking bass line as you become more comfortable with it.

Drums

Intro

Main Groove

Coda

PERFORMANCE TIPS

- Song begins with pickup notes on drums and guitar.

- Loosen snare tension to get a fuller snare buzz.

- Main groove is a laid-back double shuffle.

- For piano/guitar solo, play main groove on ride cymbal.

- Play light, simple fills at the end of the 12-bar phrases.

- Song ends with a crash on the "and" of beat 2.

Darlin' You Know I Love You

**Words and Music by
B.B. King and Jules Bihari**

Additional Lyrics

2. I think of you ev'ry morning
    And I'd remove you ev'ry night.
    And would love, love to be with you, always.

Overview

Our first blues ballad of the evening is another B.B. King tune, co-written with Jules Bihari. (This is not the last you'll see of B.B. this set!) Again, it's a traditional song, so all the instruments selected are traditional. Lyrically, the tune expresses the pain of being left behind in a relationship. "You know I love you…but you've gone and left me for someone else."

These 6/8 ballads are guaranteed crowd pleasers that let dancers sway back and forth while holding on to each other. They take the energy down a notch without putting the crowd to sleep. The trick is for the band to play very quietly, but the singer should still belt it out when the song builds up. Note the group dynamics—they will need to be rehearsed. The drummer plays a vamp that was actually used for many years in burlesque. The piano player is improvising a "honky-tonk" line all the way through the tune. The bass is the "rock" from which all other improvisation spins.

- Does the song have a swaying effect?
- Is the singer emoting with conviction?
- Get louder at end of bridge, then softer again at beginning of next verse.
- Is the vocal loud enough that you can understand the lyrics?

Section	Length	1st Chord
Intro	8 bars	G
Verse 1	8 bars	G
Verse 2	8 bars	G
Bridge	8 bars	C7
Verse 3	8 bars	G
Guitar Solo	8 bars	G
Bridge	8 bars	C7
Verse 4	13 bars	G

Lead Vocal

Range: D to G

Guitar

The "B.B. Box," Key of G

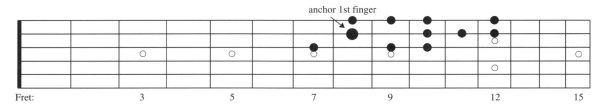

Chords

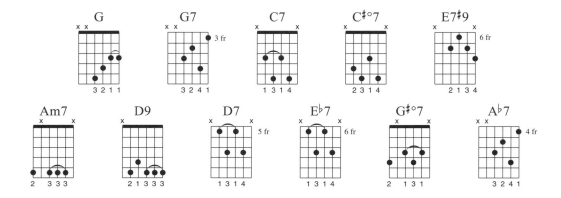

Ending

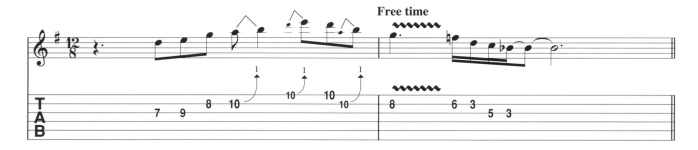

PERFORMANCE TIPS

- Use the "B.B. Box" for solos.

- Use a semi-hollowbody guitar.

- Lay low on bridge.

Keyboards

Verse

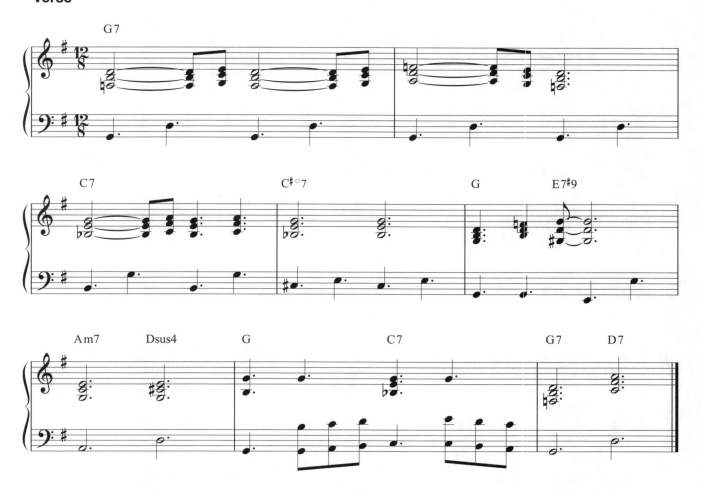

PERFORMANCE TIPS

- Use acoustic piano sound throughout.

- Play with a gospel feel.

- Add stride piano-style accents on beats 2 and 4.

- Flow with the dynamics of the group, especially in bridge.

Bass

Intro

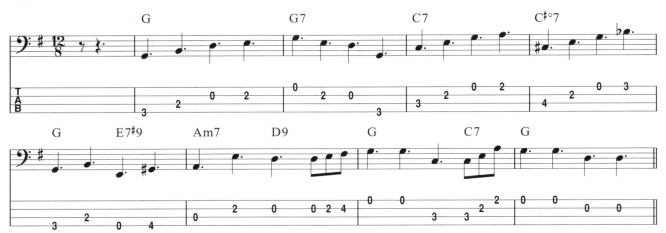

Verse Pattern

PERFORMANCE TIPS

- Stay with the smooth upright bass tone.

- Play notes long and evenly.

- Play verses quietly and tastefully, and build up to bridge.

- On bridge, keep walking and follow the chords on lead sheet; on D7/E♭7, play triplets along with drums and piano.

Drums

Intro/Bridge/Verse 4 Groove

Verse Groove

End of Bridge Buildup

Solo Groove

Ending

PERFORMANCE TIPS

- Song begins with guitar pickups.

- Play intro, bridge, and verse 4 on ride cymbal.

- Play closed hi-hat and cross-stick on verse groove.

- For buildup on end of bridge, crescendo and drag tempo until verse.

- Drummer cues free-time ending chords.

Got My Mojo Working

Words and Music by
Preston Foster

Additional Lyrics

2. I'm go'n' down to Lousiana gonna get me a mojo hand.
   I'm go'n' down to Lousiana gonna get me a mojo hand.
   I'm gonna have all you women each at my command.

Overview

"Got My Mojo Working" was written by Preston Foster, but Muddy Waters made it famous. It is actually a standard in blues circles. What is "mojo"? Usually it refers to magic powers—a spell, hex, or charm—and in some contexts it refers to sex appeal. Ironically, the song has a gospel feel, but its subject originated from pagan magic. In any case, it's one of the "exceptions"—a positive, upbeat blues tune.

This uptempo rhythm is fun for everyone to play. The drummer plays a sixteenth-note pattern with brushes for a train-like effect. The bassist is back to an electric sound, and the piano plays in tandem with the harmonica to answer the vocals. The guitarist comps all the way through. The harmonica is the featured instrument in this arrangement—if you don't have a "harpist" in the group, the part could be covered on guitar.

This is the first tune that calls for background vocals, and here they are singing in response to the melody. This is a unison "gang vocal" part with no harmony.

- Is the beat steady?
- Don't let the rest of the band drown out the sound of the drummer's brushes.
- Can you understand the lyrics?
- Are the "gang" vocals in tune?

Section	Length	1st Chord
Intro	2 bars	F7
Verse 1	12 bars	F7
Verse 2	12 bars	F7
Chorus	12 bars	F7
Harmonica Solo	12 bars	F7
Double Chorus	24 bars	F7

Lead Vocal

Range: F to A♭

Backing Vocals

Chorus

Got _____ my   mo - jo   work - in'.

PERFORMANCE TIPS

- Sing with a smile on your face (for the sake of diction).

- Use slight "slang" pronunciation ("…got my mojo *woikin'*…").

- Add some grit, especially on high notes during chorus.

Guitar

Intro

Verse/Chorus

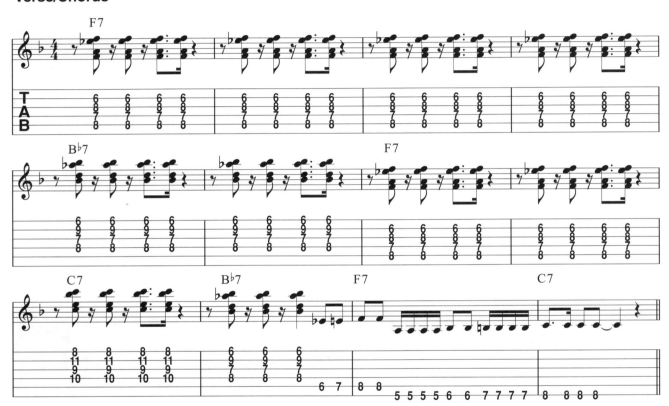

Ending

PERFORMANCE TIPS

- Use Strat-style guitar with a clean tone (no distortion).

- Attack strings hard with pick.

- If you take the solo (instead of harmonica), use the F minor pentatonic scale.

Keyboards

Left-Hand Comping Patterns

Turnaround

PERFORMANCE TIPS

- Use acoustic piano sound throughout.

- Play chords with left hand using these voicings:

- F7: 7-3-5 (E♭–A–C)

- B♭9: 3-7-9 (D–A♭–C)

- C9: 3-7-9 (E–B♭–D)

- Leave right hand free to riff.

Bass

Chorus

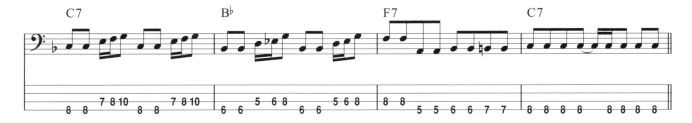

Alternate Line

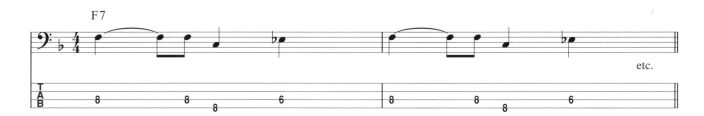

PERFORMANCE TIPS

- Play with a smooth, round tone.
- Work with the drummer to get this classic "locomotive" groove working.
- Try alternate line and see if it works well with the drums.
- Watch for the ritard ending.

Drums

Intro   **Main Groove**

Fill Into Chorus

Ending

PERFORMANCE TIPS

- Song begins with guitar pickup notes.

- Use wire brushes.

- Song is driven along by sixteenth-note main brush groove.

- Band ends together with slight ritard in last measure.

Crosscut Saw

**Words and Music by
R.G. Ford**

Intro
Moderate Blues

Verse

1. I'm a cross-cut— saw,— ba-by drag me a-cross your log.

I'm a cross-cut— saw— ba-by drag me a-cross your log.

I'll cut your wood so eas-y for you, you can't help but say, "Hot— dog."

Verse

2. Some call me Wood— Cut-tin' Sam, some call me Wood— Cut-tin' Jim. the
3. *See additional lyrics*

last girl I cut wood for she wants me — back a-gain. — I'm a cross-cut — saw, —

ba - by drag me a-cross your — log. I'll cut your

wood so eas - y for you, you can't help but say "Hot — dog, hot

Guitar Solo

dog, hot dog."

3. I got a

Coda

dog." — Whoa, — I'll cut your wood so eas - y for you,

you can't help but say "Hot — dog." —

Additional Lyrics

2. I got a double-bladed axe that really cuts 'em good.
But I'm a crosscut saw you can bury me in your wood.
I'm a crosscut saw, baby drag me across your log.
I'll cut your wood so easy for you, you can't help but say, "Hot dog."

Overview

In order to keep the set interesting and entertaining for the audience and ourselves, we're changing the feel often. Our arrangement of R.G. Ford's "Crosscut Saw" brings in a Latin influence that makes for a fun change of pace. The song is still in a 12-bar form, but the groove is close to a rhumba. Note the guitar and bass playing the same 1950's-style Latin groove. The drummer plays a traditional Latin pattern, using the snare drum as a timbale. The tom toms function as congas, and the repetitive pattern on the bass drum is reminiscent of traditional Latin percussion ensembles. The guitarist plays a Strat with real fire, connecting the tune back to its blues roots. Once again, lyrical double-entendres abound in this song; the singer likens himself to a large-toothed saw while actually bragging about his sexual prowess!

Just as in any other blues song, it's important to pay close attention to the dynamics so the singer and soloist are easily heard and understood.

- Is the drummer playing this busy pattern smoothly?
- Is the organ "padding" in support of the singer and soloist?
- Drummer and guitarist should hit accents together in the middle of guitar solo.

Section	Length	1st Chord
Intro	12 bars	A7
Verse 1	12 bars	A7
Verse 2	12 bars	A7
Guitar Solo	24 bars	A7
Verse 3/Coda	16 bars	A7

Lead Vocal

Range: G to E

Guitar

A Minor Pentatonic Scale

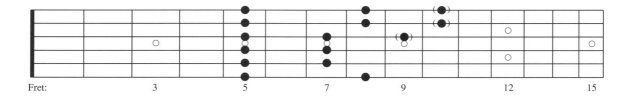

Verse Rhythm

Verse Lick

PERFORMANCE TIPS

- Use a Strat-style guitar with slight distortion.

- Attack strings hard with pick.

- Use A minor pentatonic scale for solos.

- Play "cha cha cha" ending tightly with the rest of the band.

Keyboards

Main Pattern

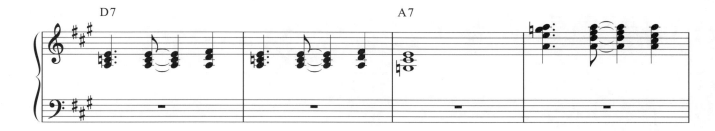

PERFORMANCE TIPS

- Use a Hammond B3 organ sound throughout.

- Use minor- to major-third grace notes on chord changes.

- Through verses 1 and 2, play legato with minimal fills.

- Get busier behind guitar solo and last verse.

- Stay tight with drummer on "cha cha cha" ending.

Bass

Verse Pattern

PERFORMANCE TIPS

- This is a fun part to play in unison with guitar; lock in and stay together.

- Make sure first note of each measure lasts for its full duration.

- Use suggested fingering for evenness of line from chord to chord.

Drums

Intro

Main Groove

Solo lead-in Fill

Solo First Ending Kicks

Solo Second Ending Fill

Ending

PERFORMANCE TIPS

- Turn snare strainer off for pseudo-timbale sound.

- Song begins with guitar pickup notes; drums enter with ride cymbal on beat one, then play main groove.

- Play main groove for entire song (with the exception of fills).

- Play kicks with guitar on first ending of guitar solo into repeat.

- Band ends together with "cha-cha-cha."

Caldonia
(What Makes Your Big Head So Hard?)

**Words and Music by
Fleecie Moore**

Additional Lyrics

2. Spoken: *You know, my mama told me to leave Caldonia alone.*
She said she's bad for my morale.
But mama doesn't know what Caldonia's been puttin' down.
So, I figured I'd just go down to Caldonia's house
And ask her just one more time…

Overview

Let's keep the mood up with another "positive blues" tune. "Caldonia," written by Fleecie Moore in 1945, was covered most prominently by jump blues artist Louis Jordan. The title refers to a woman who the singer's mother doesn't like. He asks the proverbial question, "Caldonia, what makes your big head so hard?" The song is funny and fun.

Now's the time to pull out our best jump blues groove. This swing feel is loose and fun to dance to. The drummer plays a straight-ahead swing pattern on the ride and hi-hat. Make sure the accents coming out of the intro are tight. The guitarist is back to a hollowbody, playing a solo that is idiomatically correct and accurate. The bass player also gets to step out with a slap solo! The piano part is a quarter-note comp pattern that really helps to move the groove forward. Let the singer sell the lyrics and the song to the audience with rousing delivery.

- Does the entire band play all the breaks clean and accurately?
- Can the singer be heard and understood easily?
- Do the solos sound and feel like 1950's jump blues?

Section	Length	1st Chord
Intro	24 bars	G
Verse 1	12 bars	G
Chorus	12 bars	G
Guitar Solo	36 bars	G
Bass Solo	12 bars	N.C.
Verse 2	12 bars	G
Chorus	12 bars + ending	G

Lead Vocal

Range: E to F

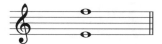

PERFORMANCE TIPS

- Sing in a big-band/jump-blues voice, smooth and rich—keep the smile on!

- Add a short slap-back delay (if available) for a "retro" sound.

- Add vibrato on held notes.

- Shout out "Caldonia!" full voice, with a little vocal gravel.

Guitar

Intro

Chords

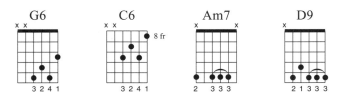

PERFORMANCE TIPS

- Use a Strat-style guitar with a clean tone.

- Solo using a hybrid G blues and G major scale approach.

- Stay tight with drummer on breaks at end of intro and song ending.

Keyboards

Intro Pattern

PERFORMANCE TIPS

- Use acoustic piano sound throughout.

- Left hand should be almost imperceptible throughout; so should both hands on beats 1 and 3.

- Later in song, left hand plays right-hand rhythm part (chords on two and four); right hand riffs.

- Add downward glisses at end of stops ("what make your big head so hard?") and end of bass solo.

- Stay tight with drums and guitar on ending.

Bass

Intro (with Second Ending)

PERFORMANCE TIPS

- Play with a big, round, upright tone.

- Play variations of intro pattern throughout, walking steadily.

- If you're playing a standup, play slap solo as on recording. If not, a melodic or walking solo on electric bass will do fine.

- Keep the tempo moving forward without rushing.

Drums

Intro Pickup

Intro/Guitar Solo Groove

Verse lead-in Lick

Verse Groove

Chorus Breaks

Guitar Solo Lead-in Fill

Bass Solo Groove

Ending Lick

PERFORMANCE TIPS

- Song begins with pickup fill on snare with guitar.

- Play bass drum softly.

- Play verse lead-in lick with band.

- On guitar solo lead-in fill, hit strong rimshots.

- Play ending lick exactly as written with band.

(They Call It) Stormy Monday
(Stormy Monday Blues)

Words and Music by
Aaron "T-Bone" Walker

Intro

Verse

1. They call it storm-y Mon-day,   but Tues - day's just

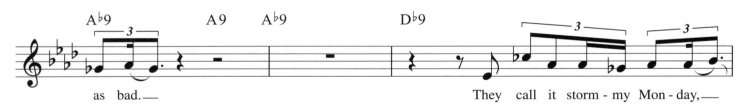

as bad.—   They call it storm - my Mon - day,—

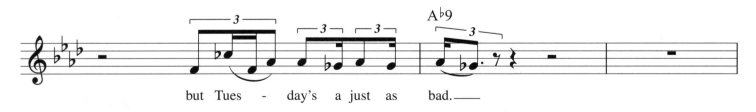

but Tues - day's a just as   bad.——

Wednes-day is worse,——   and Thurs-day's, oh, —— so sad.—

Overview

Time to bring the mood and feel back down. This jazzy blues ballad by T-Bone Walker has been done differently by almost everyone who has covered it—even Southern-rock pioneers the Allman Brothers Band did a version in the seventies. The lyrics are about the misery of lost love. "They call it Stormy Monday, but Tuesday's just as bad." By the time we make it to the end of the week, we're all feeling the blues!

Our arrangement is light and airy, with a definite jazz undertone. The drummer plays with brushes, very lightly. The guitarist is leaning towards a jazz sensibility, and the piano player comps with a loose and light approach. The piano and guitar create a "call and response" dialog between themselves and the vocalist. The bass player walks a simple quarter-note pattern, ideally on a standup bass. The guitar solo in the intro is almost dreamlike, with a light and simple approach that contrasts with, and leaves space for, the bluesy vocals.

When musicians talk about "space," they're referring to musical ideas that have been rhythmically altered and simplified to allow room for the soloist or singer. "Space" is a vital commodity when playing a jazz-blues ballad, allowing the vocalist to stylize a tune any way he or she sees fit.

- Is the entire band leaving "space" for the vocalist?
- Is the drummer staying out of the way, playing more of a pulse than a pattern?
- Is the intro tight and the figures accented gently?

Section	Length	1st Chord
Intro	26 bars	E9
Verse 1	12 bars	A♭9
Verse 2	12 bars	A♭9
Verse 3	12 bars	A♭9

Lead Vocal

Range: E♭ to G♭

PERFORMANCE TIPS

- You can drop the smile now!

- Sing in a spacious, light style with vibrato.

- Sing "way behind the beat."

- Add grit and energy on verse 3 ("Lord have mercy…").

Guitar

A♭ Blues/Major Pentatonic Scale Hybrid

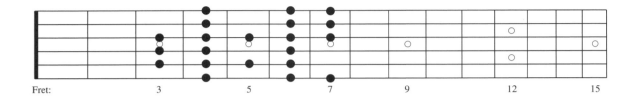

Verse 3

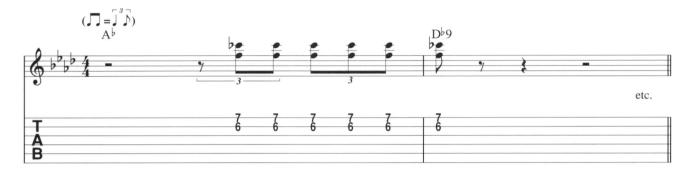

Ending

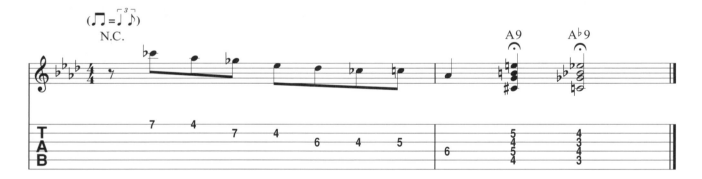

PERFORMANCE TIPS

- Use a semi-hollowbody guitar with a warm tone (pickup in neck position).

- Use A♭ blues/major pentatonic scale hybrid to improvise jazzy blues solos.

- Play spaciously under singer during verses.

- Answer the singer's dynamic phrases with fills on last verse: "Lord have mercy…"

Keyboards

Intro

Bass

Intro/Verse Pattern

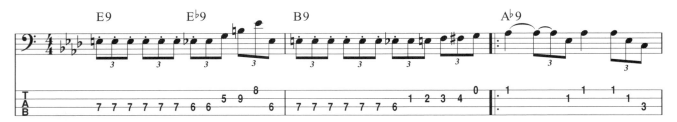

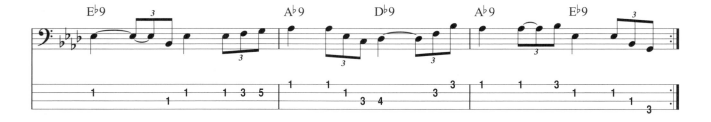

PERFORMANCE TIPS

- Practice tricky finger positions in the intro; try another fingering if it's uncomfortable.

- Play legato throughout.

- Keep triplet feel in your head for additional fills.

- Improvise and expand the part as you become more familiar with chord changes.

- You are the timekeeper here! Walk quarter notes to keep tempo from changing.

Drums

Intro Lick

Intro Groove

Verse Groove

Verse 3 Meas. 1 & 5

Ending

PERFORMANCE TIPS

- Use wire brushes.
- Play bass drum softly.
- Band plays intro lick together.
- Play intro groove with brushes on snare with ad lib fills.
- For verse, right hand plays ride cymbal.
- On ending, you cue the fermata notes.

Wang Dang Doodle

Written by Willie Dixon

Intro

Moderate Blues Rock

Verse

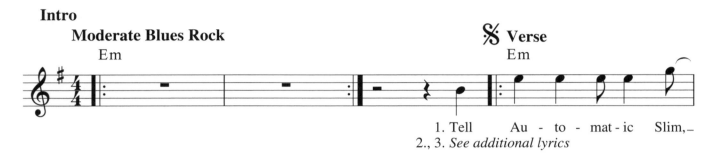

1. Tell Au - to - mat - ic Slim,—
2., 3. *See additional lyrics*

—— a tell Raz - or Tot-in' Jim.—— Tell Butch-er Knife Tot-in' An-

nie,—— a tell Fast —— Talk-in' Fan - nie. We gon-na pitch a ball,

— a down a to that a un-ion hall.—— We're gon-na romp and tromp till mid-

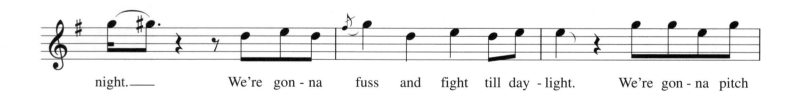

night.—— We're gon-na fuss and fight till day - light. We're gon-na pitch

a wang— dang— doo-dle all — night ———— long.——

Chorus

All night— long,—— all night— long.—— All night — long,—

To Coda

—— all night — long — We're gon-na pitch a wang—— dang——

doo-dle all—— night———————— long.—— 2. Tell ——————— long.——

Coda

—— All night— long,—— oh,———— all night — long.—

rit.

—— Heh. All——— night— long. ——

Additional Lyrics

2. Tell a Crawlin' Red, a tell Abyssinian Ned.
   Go tell ol' Pistol Pete, a tell everybody he meets.
   Tonight we need no rest. We're gonna really throw a mess.
   We're gonna knock down a all the windows,
   We're gonna kick down all the doors.
   We're gonna pitch a wang dang doodle all night long.

3. Tell Fats, and Washboard Sam, a tell a everybody gonna jam.
   A tell Shakin' Boxcar Joe we got a sawdust a on the floor.
   Tell Peg and Caroline Dim we're gonna have a heck of a time.
   And when the fish scent fills the air,
   There'll be a stump juice a ev'rywhere, well.
   A we gonna pitch a wang dang doodle all night long.

Overview

It's time to kick things back into high gear with a driving "positive blues" tune. "Wang Dang Doodle," originally by Willie Dixon, is a signature song for Koko Taylor, the Queen of the Blues. Howlin' Wolf gave us the definitive version, and it was also an unlikely live cover tune for the Grateful Dead! The song has a strange cadence but a tremendous groove. The lyrics are about a huge party and a big party attitude. "We're gonna pitch a Wang Dang Doodle all night long!"

The drums grind out a driving groove. The bass follows suit with the identifying hook. The guitar, acting as a support instrument, plays the riff along with the bass after the short intro. The lead vocals are aggressive, telling the story of characters from the neighborhood partying and raising the roof. The low background vocals reinforce the difference between sections and add dynamics to the story.

- Is the bass loud enough to carry the signature line?
- Is the drummer steady?
- Verse 1 starts at an unpredictable time: what seems to be "halfway through" the repeating bass figure.

Section	Length	1st Chord
Intro	5 bars	Em
Verse 1	20 bars	Em
Chorus	12 bars	Em
Verse 2	20 bars	Em
Chorus	12 bars	Em
Verse 3	20 bars	Em
Chorus	16 bars	Em

Lead Vocal

Range: E to B

Backing Vocals

Chorus

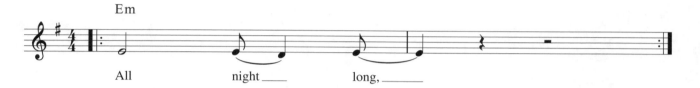

All   night _____   long, _____

PERFORMANCE TIPS

- Sing full-voice throughout.

- Add shaky vibrato, grit, and attitude.

- Know when to start singing: count four measures, come in on beat 4 of measure 5 (a measure off from what you might expect)!

- Add soulful "melismas" at end of verse ("We're gonna pitch a wang dang doodle all night *long*").

- Chorus covers full range of vocals; practice your pitch on high and low notes.

- Repetitive backing vocals should be dark and hypnotic.

Guitar

Intro

Drop D Tuning:
(low to high) D–A–D–G–B–E

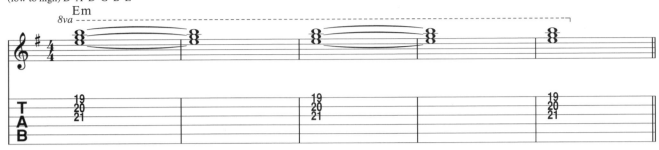

Main Riff

Drop D Tuning:
(low to high) D–A–D–G–B–E

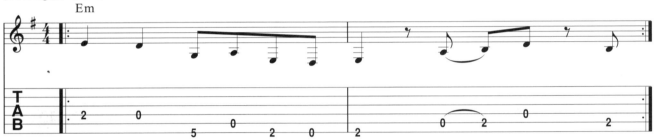

Chorus Lick

Drop D Tuning:
(low to high) D–A–D–G–B–E

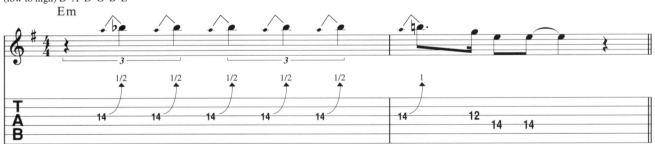

PERFORMANCE TIPS

- Use Strat-style guitar with a clean tone.

- Use drop D tuning; make sure you're in tune with bass.

- Play chorus lick to answer vocalist at the end of phrase: "We're gonna pitch a wang dang doodle all night long."

- Get louder near ending.

Keyboards

Chorus

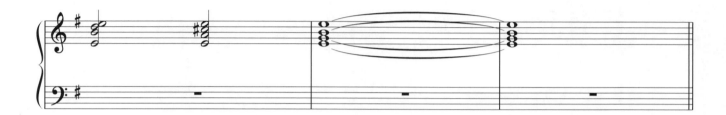

PERFORMANCE TIPS

- Use a Hammond B3 sound throughout.

- Lay out on verses.

- Come in with upward glissando into high seventh chord on chorus.

- Play lower variations of seventh chord on repeating choruses.

Bass

Intro/Main Pattern

Drop D Tuning:
(low to high) D–A–D–G

PERFORMANCE TIPS

- Tune E string down to D.

- Be sure to play in the groove with drummer.

- Use a rich, full electric bass tone.

- Keep the song moving—don't slow down the tempo.

- Your bass line is the foundation of this song; play solid and strong.

Drums

Main Groove

Sample Fill #1

Sample Fill #2

Sample Fill #3

Ending

rit.

PERFORMANCE TIPS

- Full band starts together.

- Play main groove throughout.

- Play fills leading into verses and choruses.

- For Coda, play half-open hi-hat to drive the the groove until the end.

- On ending, cue ritard.

I'm Tore Down

**Words and Music by
Sonny Thompson**

Intro

Chorus

I'm tore down. I'm al - most lev - el with the

ground._____ I'm tore down. I'm

al - most lev - el with the ground._____ Why____ do I____

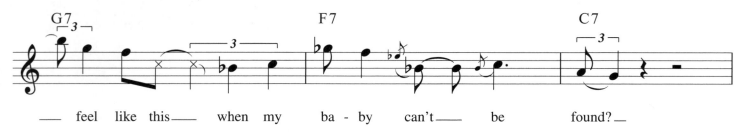

____ feel like this____ when my ba - by can't____ be found?____

Verse

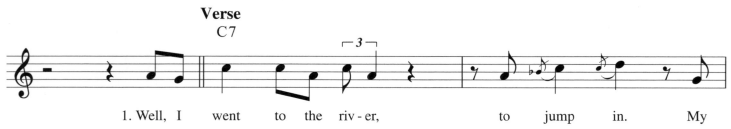

1. Well, I went to the riv - er, to jump in. My

Chorus

ba - by showed up and said, "I will tell you when." Then I'm tore down. I'm

al - most lev - el with the ground._____ Why___ do I___

— feel like this ___ when my ba - by can't ___ be found?___

Verse

2. I love you ba - by with my heart and soul. _____
3. *See additional lyrics*

Love like___ mine___ will nev - er grow old. I love you in the morn - in' and the

eve - nin' too. Ev - 'ry time you leave me I get mad at you.___ Be - cause I'm

Chorus

tore down. I'm al - most lev - el with the ground._____

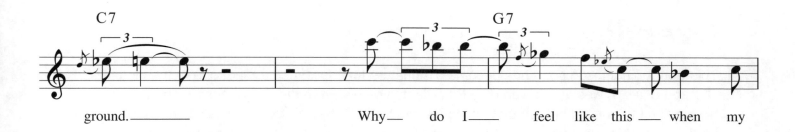

ground._____   Why__   do I__   feel like this __ when   my

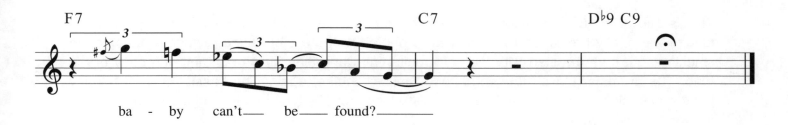

ba - by   can't__ be__ found?_____

Additional Lyrics

3   Well, I love you baby with a all my might.
    Love like mine is outta sight.
    I'll lie for you if you want me to.
    I really don't believe that your love is true.
    Because I'm tore down…

Overview

This Sonny Thompson song has become a signature tune for Freddie King, one of the pioneers of Chicago Blues. It was also covered by Eric Clapton on his *From the Cradle* album. The singer loves his woman but doesn't believe that she loves him back. "Why do I feel like this when my baby can't be found?" I think we know why: it's a blues song, and she's inevitably "stepping out on him," that's why! Lyrically, the song is "true blues," but the shuffle feel keeps it upbeat.

This is one of the most challenging songs to sing, but with great returns. The catchy shuffle is loaded with funky breaks and fun devices to pull off with the other band members. It comes in smoking right from the start with the quick guitar intro and then jumps right into the body of the tune. The drummer plays that two-handed "double shuffle" again. The bassist plays a bouncy pattern that mirrors the drummer's. The pianist's loose honky-tonk part is the glue that helps hold the whole thing together.

- Are the verse breaks tight and snappy?
- Is the piano playing with a honky-tonk feel, and not clashing with the vocals?
- Are the bass and drums shuffling with the same feel and groove?

Section	Length	1st Chord
Intro	4 bars	G7
Chorus	12 bars	C7
Verse 1	4 bars	C7
Chorus	8 bars	F7
Verse 2	8 bars	C7
Chorus	8 bars	F7
Guitar Solo	24 bars	C7
Verse 3	8 bars	C7
Chorus	8 bars	F7
Outro-Chorus	12 bars	C7

Lead Vocal

Range: G to C

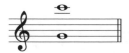

PERFORMANCE TIPS

- Sing in a light, easygoing, Clapton-esque voice.

- Sing right on the beat, especially on verse stops.

- High C note in chorus ("*Why* do I feel like this…") is falsetto; practice staying on pitch while transitioning between natural and falsetto voice.

Guitar

Intro

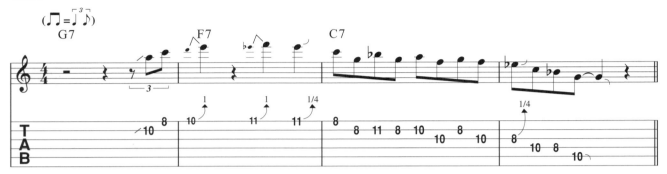

Chorus Riffs

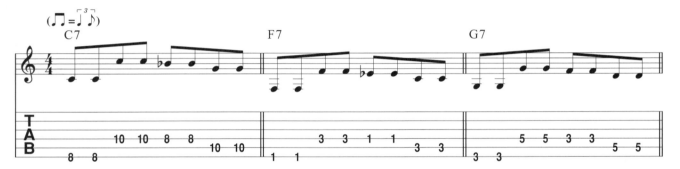

Chorus Lick 1

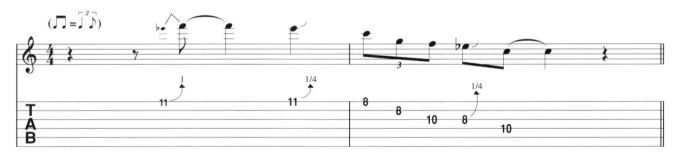

Chorus Lick 2

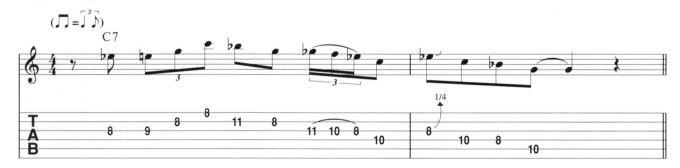

PERFORMANCE TIPS

- Play chorus riffs along with the bass, and add chorus licks in between vocal phrases.

- Play solo using the C minor pentatonic scale.

- Note that second and third breaks in verses are longer than the first.

Keyboards

Example Chorus Pattern

PERFORMANCE TIPS

- Use acoustic piano sound throughout.

- Work left and right hands into steady comping pattern.

- Keep left hand softer.

- Stay tight with drummer on verse stops.

- Add downward glissandos and trills on transition from verse to chorus.

- Move pattern up an octave and add extra fills on outro-chorus.

Bass

Chorus

Ending

PERFORMANCE TIPS

- Watch out for stop time.
- Keep the bouncy line moving; don't drag.
- Nail the ending with the rest of the band.

Drums

Intro

Chorus Groove   **Verse 1**

Sample Long Verse

Solo Groove   **Ending**

PERFORMANCE TIPS

- Song begins with drum pickup.

- Loosen snare tension to get a fuller snare buzz.

- Play chorus groove on half-open hi-hat.

- Verse 1 is four bars; verses 2 and 3 are eight bars each.

- Outro chorus is extended 1 measure plus ending lick; let cymbals ring.

The Thrill Is Gone

**Words and Music by
Roy Hawkins and Rick Darnell**

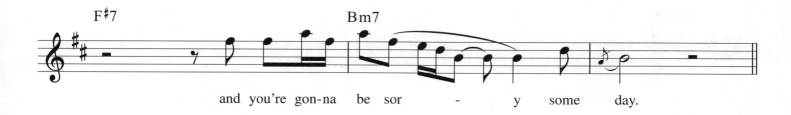

and you're gon-na be sor - y some day.

Verse

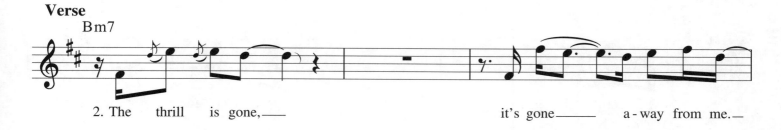

2. The thrill is gone,___ it's gone___ a - way from me.___

___ Oh,___ the thrill is gone,___ pret - ty ba - by,

the thrill is gone___ a - way from me. And al - though I___ still___ live___

on, but so lone - ly I will___ be.___

Guitar Solo

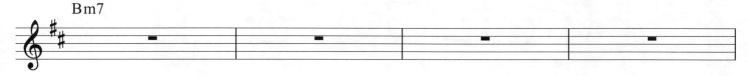

Overview

"The Thrill Is Gone" is a signature ballad for B.B. King. Written by Rick Darnell and Roy Hawkins in 1951, it's probably the most famous minor blues ballad in history. This is a great second-to-last song for the set because, hopefully, the crowd has settled in and is listening to the band. Such a heart-wrenching ballad, delivered with conviction, will entice the crowd into staying for more. Lyrically, the song tells a story of real heartbreak. Anyone who has gone through a tough breakup knows the universal feeling expressed in "The Thrill Is Gone."

The guitar carries the show from intro to solo and in the outro. Clean semi-hollowbody sounds, played with real feel, will make this tune tick. The lead vocals should be delivered with soul and conviction in order to do justice to B.B. The drums and bass stay supportive with a simple but effective groove. The band's dynamics must be strong to play this song well. It's very repetitive, so we must rely on dynamics and strong vocals to bring the feeling across.

- Does the singer deliver a sad, dark performance that is believable?
- Is the guitar subdued until the last solo and ending?
- Is the piano choosing voicings that help support the guitarist and vocalist?
- Does the band dynamic change from verse to verse?

Section	Length	1st Chord
Intro	12 bars	Bm7
Verse 1	12 bars	Bm7
Verse 2	12 bars	Bm7
Guitar Solo	12 bars	Bm7
Verse 3	12 bars	Bm7
Verse 4	12 bars	Bm7
Outro-Guitar Solo	16 bars	Bm7

Lead Vocal

Range: F# to A

Guitar

Intro Solo

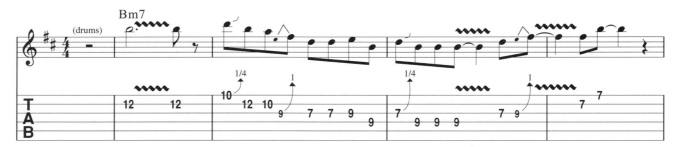

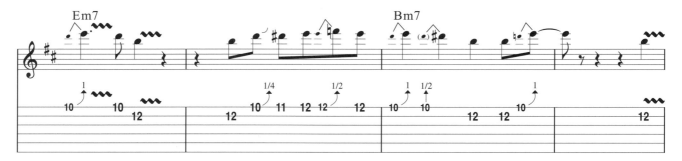

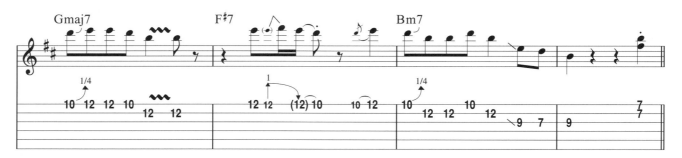

B Minor Pentatonic Scale

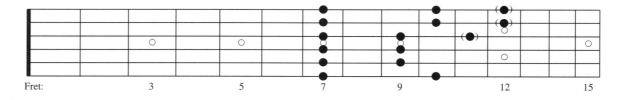

Fret: 3   5   7   9   12   15

Chords

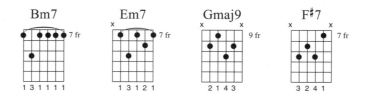

PERFORMANCE TIPS

- Use a semi-hollowbody guitar with a bright, clean tone.

- Play solos sensitively, using the B minor pentatonic scale shown.

- Strum chords gently and sparsely in verses.

Keyboards

Verse Pattern

PERFORMANCE TIPS

- Use electric piano sound throughout, or combine acoustic and electric sounds.

- Use legato chording and arpeggios to add elegance.

- Use lots of sustain pedal.

Bass

Intro/Verse

PERFORMANCE TIPS

- Play with fingers close to neck for a fat tone.

- Dial in a large sound with lots of bass.

- Play notes evenly.

- Don't rush the tempo; play somewhat behind the beat.

Drums

Intro Pickup

Main Groove

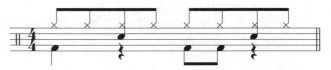

Sample Fill #1

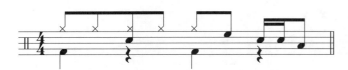

Sample Fill #2

Outro-Guitar Solo Groove

Ending

PERFORMANCE TIPS

- Song begins with drum pickup.

- Play main groove on closed hi-hat.

- Play laid back in pocket with bass player.

- Play simple, tasteful fills.

- For outro guitar solo, play main groove on ride cymbal.

- Free-time ending cued by guitarist.

- After last crash hit, play cymbal bells during fermata for embellishment.

Boom Boom

Words and Music by
John Lee Hooker

Overview

Time for some more "positive blues" to round off the set. "Boom Boom" is an absolute smoker, to be played and sung with extra added dirt. No one sings this song like its writer, John Lee Hooker, though many have tried—his gravel and feel are second to none. This one hardly ever fails to pack the dance floor, and that's the way we want to leave the set. Address this song with as much punch as you can muster.

Once again, the lyrics are about animal attraction; "Boom Boom" isn't referring to the sound of a bass drum. (Do we see a theme developing here?) Appropriately, the song's energy is up all the way through. Even with two guitar solos, it's a short song, and that's another reason it makes a good closing number. Play the guitar loud and hard. The bassist and drummer should attack like rock players while holding on to that blues-shuffle feel. Now let it roll. Have fun, and your audience will too!

- Are the breaks tight?
- Is the singer selling the raw energy that is this song?
- Are the dynamics in place when the singer sings?
- Kick in hard on the guitar solos!

Section	Length	1st Chord
Intro	12 bars	E5
Chorus	8 bars	E5
Verse 1	12 bars	E5
Chorus	12 bars	E5
Guitar Solo	23 bars	E5
Chorus	8 bars	E5
Verse 2	12 bars	E5
Chorus	12 bars	E5
Outro-Guitar Solo	24 bars	E5

Lead Vocal

Range: E to E (2 Octaves!)

PERFORMANCE TIPS

- Sing low with plenty of vocal gravel.

- Add some vibrato on "Boom, boom, boom, boom."

- If you can't hit the low E, sing it an octave or a fifth (B) higher.

- Note the extreme contrast in range and dynamics between "How how how how" and "Hey, yay, yeah!"

Guitar

Intro

Verse

E Blues Scale

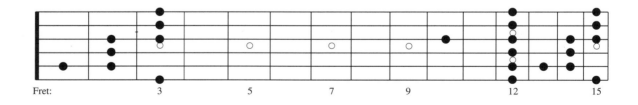

Fret: 3   5   7   9   12   15

PERFORMANCE TIPS

- Use E blues scale (shown in 2 positions) for solos.

- Dial in slight gritty distortion.

- Stay tight with the drummer on verse/chorus breaks.

Keyboards

Chorus

Guitar Solo

PERFORMANCE TIPS

- Use a dirty Hammond B3 sound with distortion.

- Let guitar and bass drive the song.

- Answer guitar riffs along with drums.

- Use higher chords during guitar solo.

Bass

Verse

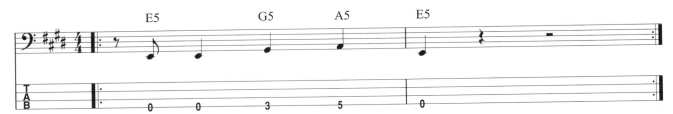

Solos

PERFORMANCE TIPS

- Play meanly!

- A rough tone with fret noise can add to this song's flavor.

- Keep eye contact with other players to help nail the unison parts.

Drums

Intro

Chorus/Verse Lick

Guitar Solo Lead-in Fill

Guitar Solo Groove

Ending

PERFORMANCE TIPS

- Song begins with guitar and quarter-note kick drum.

- For chorus and verse, play two-measure lick repeated.

- Play ride cymbal on guitar solo groove.

- Fill leading back to verse is same as ending fill.

- Choke crash cymbal on ending.

GIG GUIDES

These unique books are laid out with performance in mind. The setlist we have included reflects a wide selection of the most accessible, "field-tested" material available, arranged for a four-piece band in a sequence that's meant to keep your audience entertained. Use it in rehearsal and performance, following along with the lead sheets and individual parts. Each song in the set includes:

- A lead sheet with chords, melody, and lyrics
- An intro page with song facts, song form, and performance tips for the full band
- A page of guidelines for each bandmember, including crucial parts and performance tips for vocals, guitar, keyboards, bass, and drums.
- Each song is fully demonstrated on the accompanying CD.

Song intro pages contain some information that might be useful to the frontperson as between-song banter: the story behind the song, when and by whom it was recorded, and so on. Parts and performance tips are written by professional musicians with field experience (not just some guy in a cubicle). If all bandmembers follow their parts in the book and the accompanying CD, and the band rehearses well, you will be gig-ready in no time.

FOR MORE INFORMATION, SEE YOUR LOCAL MUSIC DEALER, OR WRITE TO:

HAL•LEONARD®
CORPORATION

7777 W. BLUEMOUND RD. P.O. BOX 13819 MILWAUKEE, WI 53213

www.halleonard.com

Prices, contents and availability subject to change without notice.

WEDDING FIRST SET
12 songs: Wonderful Tonight • My Girl • Georgia on My Mind • Rock Around the Clock • Blue Suede Shoes • Desafinado (Off Key) • Tennessee Waltz • Save the Last Dance for Me • Misty • In the Mood • Could I Have This Dance • I Saw Her Standing There.
00699256 Book/CD Pack $19.95

WEDDING SECOND SET
Includes a dozen songs to get wedding guests in a party mood: Another One Bites the Dust • Daddy's Little Girl • Happy Together • La Bamba • Limbo Rock • Mustang Sally • Never Gonna Let You Go • Silhouettes • The Stripper • Tequila • Twist and Shout • Wooly Bully.
00699257 Book/CD Pack $19.95

WEDDING THIRD SET
Features 12 more popular favorites in a variety of styles: Beer Barrel Polka (Roll Out the Barrel) • Brick House • 867-5309/Jenny • (Everything I Do) I Do It for You • Friends in Low Places • Great Balls of Fire • The House Is Rockin' • Shout • Stand by Me • Takin' Care of Business • What I Like About You • Y.M.C.A.
00699258 Book/CD Pack $19.95

BLUES SET
12 songs: Born Under a Bad Sign • Killing Floor • Rock Me Baby • Darlin', You Know I Love You • I Got My Mojo Working • Crosscut Saw • Caldonia (What Makes Your Big Head So Hard) • (They Call It) Stormy Monday (Stormy Monday Blues) • Wang Dang Doodle • I'm Tore Down • The Thrill Is Gone • Boom Boom.
00310786 Book/CD Pack $19.95

DISCO SET
12 songs: Love Rollercoaster • Stayin' Alive • That's the Way I Like It • You Make Me Feel Like Dancing • Super Freak • Y.M.C.A. • Pick Up the Pieces • Brick House • Shadow Dancing • You Should be Dancing • Get Down Tonight • Macho Man.
00699259 Book/CD Pack $19.95

PRAISE & WORSHIP SET
12 songs: He Has Made Me Glad • He Is Exalted • All Hail King Jesus • Awesome God • Glorify Thy Name • As the Deer • We Bring A Sacrifice of Praise • Lord I Lift Your Name On High • Majesty • Shout the Lord • I Love You Lord • Give Thanks • Instrumental mixes.
00842056 Book/CD Pack $19.95